Feathers
in the Wind

Feathers
in the Wind
Sally Grindley

BLOOMSBURY
LONDON NEW DELHI NEW YORK SYDNEY

Bloomsbury Publishing, London, New Delhi, New York and Sydney

First published in Great Britain in September 2012 by Bloomsbury Publishing Plc
50 Bedford Square, London, WC1B 3DP

Manufactured and supplied under licence from the Zoological Society of London

Licensed by Bright Group International
www.thebrightagency.com

With thanks to ZSL's conservation team

A CIP catalogue record for this book is available from the British Library

ISBN 978 1 4088 1947 0

MIX
Paper from
responsible sources
FSC® C020471

Typeset by Hewer Text UK Ltd, Edinburgh
Printed and bound in Great Britain by CPI Group (UK) Ltd, Croydon, CR0 4YY

1 3 5 7 9 10 8 6 4 2

www.storiesfromthezoo.com
www.bloomsbury.com
www.sallygrindley.co.uk

For Thomas Sellick

Chapter 1

'Vultures!' Aesha pulled a face. 'Why would we go all the way to India to hang out with vultures? They're ugly and disgusting.' She pushed her dinner plate away as though it contained something distasteful.

'They speak very highly of you too,' her father, Peter, replied.

'I think they're rather handsome,' said her mother. 'And they fulfil a very vital role.'

'Like scavenging on things that other animals have killed,' Aesha said scornfully.

'That's exactly right,' said Binti. 'They clean up what's been left, and that's very important

1

in helping to prevent disease. Talking of which, it's your turn to clear the table.'

'What's India like?' Joe asked.

Their mother, Binti, who was an international vet, had just announced that they were going to spend time there while she helped with research into why vulture numbers were declining to such an extent that they were becoming endangered.

'It's hot and noisy and chaotic and full of wonderful smells and there's an amazing photo to be taken every few seconds,' Peter told him.

Joe perked up at the idea of that. He had his very own camera and wanted to follow in his father's footsteps as a wildlife photographer.

'So why are vultures in India endangered?' Aesha wanted to know. 'We saw lots of them when we were in Africa.'

'It seems they may be sensitive to a drug used to treat cattle,' Binti replied.

'Vultures don't eat cattle, do they?' said Joe.

'Yes, they do,' said Binti. 'When cattle die,

farmers take their carcasses to a communal place and leave them for vultures and other scavengers to pick over. Traces of the drug have been found in some carcasses, and there appears to be a link between that and the dramatic reduction in vulture numbers.'

'So they need to stop using the drug,' said Aesha. 'Job done.' She pushed back her chair and collected the dirty plates.

'If only it were that simple,' said Binti. 'Farmers rely on certain drugs to keep their cattle healthy. And cattle are vital to the farmers' livelihoods.'

'It's never simple, is it, Mum?' Joe commented.

Foggy the dog woke from his slumber under the table and nestled his head on Joe's knee.

'So many things depend on other things, don't they, Foggy?' he continued.

'Upset one cog in a finely tuned engine and the whole lot grinds to a halt,' his father agreed. 'It's the same with the natural world, and it's

3

usually man's interference that causes the problem.'

'Sometimes human beings are so dumb. We do so much damage to the world around us.' Aesha sounded as if she'd rather not be human. Joe often wondered if she was an alien rather than his sister.

'Sometimes a perfectly innocent pursuit can cause problems,' said Binti. 'One of the things that's not helping the vulture population in India is kite-flying. That's the main reason for my trip.'

'Kite-flying!' Joe was incredulous. 'How can kite-flying affect vultures?'

'It probably scares them!' said Aesha.

'It's worse than that. January the fourteenth is the annual International Kite Festival in Ahmedabad, where we're staying. Everyone flies kites to celebrate Uttarayan – the end of winter and beginning of summer,' Binti explained. 'They cover the strings of the kites with ground glass, which makes them sharp.

The idea is that kite-flyers target rival kites and try to cut them out of the sky. Sadly, large numbers of vultures get caught up in the strings.'

Joe grimaced at the thought of what could happen to the vultures.

'Mum, that's awful!' Aesha cried. 'Surely not many vultures would fly into them, would they?'

'Yes, unfortunately – especially since the festival covers such a huge area,' said Peter. 'Your mother will be helping to save the injured birds while we're there.'

Joe looked at his mother with pride. Not only did his mother come from Tanzania, which meant he was half-African, but he and Aesha were lucky enough to travel the world because of their parents' professions. *It's so cool having an international vet for a mum*, he thought.

Chapter 2

The next few days passed in a whirl as Joe and his family prepared themselves for their trip. Joe was excited about all the opportunities he would have to take photographs, and the more he thought about the kite festival, the more he wanted his own kite to fly.

'I wouldn't want to put glass on the string because of the vultures, but it would be so cool to fly a kite with everyone else,' he said to his mother and father, hoping they would agree and buy him one.

'By the time we've packed all of your sister's ninety-two different outfits,' said Peter, 'there won't be a millimetre of extra space left in the cases for a kite.'

Aesha shot him a withering look. 'It's your cameras that take up all the space,' she countered. 'I don't know why you have to have so many of them.'

'So that I can record every single moment of my beautiful daughter's life.' Peter grinned at her. 'Even when her face resembles that of a wicked witch.'

'Careful, Dad.' Joe giggled. 'She might turn you into a frog!' He squatted on the floor and began to leap around making croaking noises. Foggy, woken from his sleep, scuffled round him, barking excitedly.

'Ha, ha, very funny,' said Aesha scornfully. 'A stone rather than a frog would be better in the case of annoying little boys.'

'If you don't all get a move on, you'll have more than a wicked witch after you,' threatened Binti.

'Come on, Joe,' said Peter, opening the front

7

door and calling Foggy to heel. 'Let's flee the coven before things turn really nasty.'

'Poor Foggy,' said Joe. 'Off to the doggery again.' He patted him on the head as they got into the car.

'Most dogs in India would give their back teeth to go where Foggy's going,' said Peter. 'A plump mattress to sleep on, doggy biscuits in all sorts of flavours, bones with meat on, lots of pats and hugs and walkies, and lady friends to make him feel like a prize pooch. Poor Foggy!'

Joe pouted. 'I know,' he said, 'but it's not the same as being at home.'

'Most dogs in India don't have a home,' Peter replied. He tooted his horn at a motorist who had cut in sharply in front of them, making Joe jump. 'There'll be plenty of that in India,' he added, tooting the horn again for good measure.

Joe felt sorry for the dogs in India. At the same time he was uneasy about coming across them in the streets. 'Are they dangerous?' he asked.

'The dogs or the motorists?' Peter chuckled. 'Actually, they're both as bad, but the dogs will be more interested in scavenging through rubbish than taking bites out of skinny little boys, though they can be quite scary and some of them carry rabies. As for the motorists, they're very good at driving five-abreast along a three-lane street. You have to be sure to breathe in, that's all.'

They arrived at the boarding kennels and said their goodbyes to Foggy, who trotted off happily enough as soon as he spotted another dog in the distance.

Their last stop was Peter's favourite photographic shop, where he stocked up on equipment to take the amazing wildlife photographs that hung on the walls of their house and appeared in newspapers and magazines. Joe gazed enthusiastically at the cabinets and shelves with their displays of cameras in all shapes and sizes, as well as lenses and leads, cases and batteries. There was so much more to taking a photograph than pointing a camera and pressing a button.

As they left the shop, Peter handed Joe a small package. 'It's a zoom lens for your camera,' he said. 'You'll need it for photographing those kites.'

Chapter 3

It hadn't occurred to Joe that he would have his first curry of their Indian trip on board the plane to Delhi. He liked curry, as long as it wasn't too hot. His father was 'a dab hand' at cooking Asian food and Joe loved to help him blend and grind down spices in their pestle and mortar, breathing in the delicious spicy smells until they made him sneeze. For a special treat their parents would take Aesha and him to their local Indian restaurant, where he always chose chicken tikka.

Joe lifted the foil lid on the meal in front of him, unsure whether he was going to like it or not. It didn't look particularly appetising in its plastic container.

'You'll have to get used to eating curry for breakfast, lunch and dinner,' said Peter, grinning at him. 'Of course, it won't be as good as mine.'

'What if it's too hot?' Joe wanted to know.

'We'll make sure you don't choose anything that will blow the roof of your mouth off,' his father replied. 'Eat up now or you'll be saying it's too cold.'

Joe took a bite of the meat and was pleased to find that it was a lot tastier than most airline food. He ate the lot. One mouthful of the pudding was enough, though, because to him it tasted like his mother's perfume!

'Will we really have to have curry for breakfast?' he asked her.

'I'm sure there'll be an alternative in the hotel,' said Binti. 'Much as I love curry, even I would struggle to eat it three times a day.'

'I hope they have cereal,' Aesha piped up.

Joe had mixed feelings about staying in a hotel. On previous trips, he and his family had often been housed with local conservationists in their staff headquarters, as they had, for instance, when they visited eastern Russia to help with a project to save tigers. The staff headquarters were very basic, but being there had made Joe feel part of the team. When they stayed in a hotel, he felt more like a tourist and less involved, despite the fact that it was much more comfortable.

'Is there a swimming pool at the hotel?' he asked, though it was Aesha who was the swimming champion in the family.

'Only for toddlers,' Peter responded, winking at Joe.

'What!' Aesha exclaimed. 'What about the regional championships in two months' time? Mum, you promised we'd stay somewhere with a pool.'

'Don't listen to your father. He's pulling your leg,' Binti reassured her. 'Not only is there a pool, but there's a gym as well, though you won't be allowed to use it at your age.'

'Dad will be able to run off his big fat belly,' said Joe, giggling loudly.

'You leave my belly out of it,' retorted Peter. 'It's a perfect specimen and much loved, thank you.'

'A perfect specimen of what happens when you enjoy your food too much,' said Aesha.

'He'd probably break the running machine, wouldn't he, Mum?' Joe squealed with laughter.

Peter patted his stomach. 'Let them mock,' he said. 'We know where true happiness lies.'

Joe leant his head against his mother's shoulder. 'Will I be able to help with the injured vultures?' he asked.

'They might be a bit of a sorry sight,' Binti replied.

'Do they just fall from the sky when the kites injure them?'

'I suppose some might. Others will try to keep flying until they find somewhere safe to land.' Binti squeezed his hand. 'Sometimes it's very difficult for humans and animals to live side by side, yet we're so very dependent upon each other. Nobody wants the vultures to be hurt, but the kite festival is an important tradition.'

Joe closed his eyes. He started to imagine a sky full of kites in a multitude of colours, shapes and sizes, dancing merrily in the breeze. Some of them had faces, smiling faces. He smiled back at them. Gradually, the breeze grew stronger, turning into a powerful wind. The faces began to change. The kites began to whip and snap. The wind became a howling gale and the faces grew stern, then angry. Suddenly, the sky was filled with feathers, brown, white and grey, and speckled among them were eyes wide with fear. The kites swooped and swept through the feathers, tearing them apart, until they were powerless to resist such force and plummeted to the ground. There they shivered and fretted in forlorn heaps, while the kites, smiling once more, danced again in the breeze.

When Joe woke, he didn't know where he was for a moment and felt unaccountably anxious.

'Not long now,' his mother said. 'They're about to bring some food and then we'll be preparing to land.'

'I don't think I want to watch the kites,' he murmured.

Binti looked at him questioningly, and then said reassuringly, 'We'll enjoy the festival because it's a wonderful event and we're very lucky to be able to join in the celebrations. We'll do our best for the vultures too. It's in everybody's interest to keep the vulture population healthy.'

Joe nodded and cheered up. 'Can I have my own kite then?' he asked again.

Chapter 4

One flight was followed swiftly by another from Delhi to Ahmedabad, but at last the Brook family were on the ground and making their way through passport control. *Dad was right*, Joe thought as soon as they had collected their luggage, walked through the arrivals hall and out into the street. *It is hot and noisy and chaotic!* They had been met by a driver, who was waving a piece of paper that read, *Mrs Bindu Brook*, much to Joe's amusement. The driver, who introduced himself as Ravi and said he would be looking after them during their stay, loaded their bags on to a trolley then wove his way haphazardly through queues of waiting traffic towards a crowded car park. He stopped by a big black car that looked, Joe thought, like something out of a gangster movie.

'It's an old Wolseley!' exclaimed Peter. 'They don't make them like that any more.'

He walked all round the car, stroking the bonnet and peering inside.

'It's got a walnut dashboard and velour seats. It's beautiful,' he said. 'Do you mind if I take a photo?'

Joe watched Ravi nod eagerly and blossom with pride.

'I am honoured for you to take a photo, sir,' the driver said.

'What's so exciting about a car?' Aesha asked. 'There are millions of them.'

'Ah, but not like this,' Peter replied. 'They're a rarity now. Besides, it'll remind us of our first journey on Indian soil.'

They waited while he retrieved his camera from its case and took several shots of the car from different angles, one of them with Ravi posing next to it.

When they got into the car at last, Joe gazed out of the window, looking forward to the adventure that was about to begin. From the minute they set off, however, he found himself shrinking towards his sister, who was sitting in the middle, as cars and lorries hurtled along just centimetres away from them.

'They drive so close together!' Aesha exclaimed.

'The horn rules, I think,' said Peter. 'Hold on to your hats!'

They must have loads of accidents, Joe thought, watching a car squeeze in between an autorickshaw and a truck.

'You are safe with me,' said Ravi. 'You are here for the kites?'

'We're here for the vultures,' Binti replied.

Ravi looked back at her in the mirror, a puzzled expression on his face. 'The vultures?' he repeated.

'My wife is a vet,' Peter told him. 'She's come to help save vultures that are injured by the kites.'

'You come all the way from England to help our vultures?' The driver was impressed. 'I've lived all my life in Ahmedabad and I did not know that our kites are injuring vultures.'

'They're an endangered species,' Joe blurted out.

Aesha elbowed him in the ribs and mouthed at him to shush. He glared at her. *What's wrong with saying that?* he thought.

Binti explained the different reasons for the decline in vulture numbers.

Ravi became very thoughtful and then asked, 'Do you think our kite festival is wrong – that we should stop it?'

Binti shook her head. 'Of course not,' she said. 'It's an important tradition. But it's also important that we minimise the impact on the vulture population now they've become so vulnerable.'

'We can't wait to see the kites,' added Joe. 'Dad and I are going to take lots of photos.' He was keen to make sure the driver hadn't thought he was being critical previously.

'My boy, he is like you – he cannot wait for the festival to begin. The day after tomorrow, we go to the shops and we buy his kite for him. You should go there too. There are many, many to choose from. But perhaps you are too afraid for the vultures.'

'We'll see,' said Peter, glancing round at Joe. 'We'll certainly have a look.'

'You let me know and I will take you,' Ravi replied. 'It will be my great pleasure.'

They had arrived at the hotel, which had numerous pillars holding up an extensive canopy over the main entrance. A multitude of coloured lights made it stand out imperiously against the darkening night sky. Joe was struck by how grand it was. He hadn't expected that, even if his parents had told him it had a pool and a gym. They were greeted by a doorman, sporting a large white turban and a long red coat with yellow braiding, who arranged for a porter to take their bags from Ravi, and ushered them through a revolving door into a huge reception area clad in marble and gold.

'Cool!' Aesha gasped. 'Better than staff headquarters any day.'

'It's called the Palace. You'll feel at home here, princess,' Peter said, winking at her.

Aesha groaned. 'You're so boring, Dad,' she said.

'But while I hold the purse strings, you'll have to be nice to me,' he responded.

'It's just like a palace, isn't it?' said Joe, who had been gazing around in awe. 'Look at all those statues.'

'They're Hindu gods and goddesses.' Binti walked towards them and pointed at one that resembled a monkey. 'This one here is called Hanuman and is worshipped as a symbol of physical strength and perseverance. The one with the elephant head is Ganesha, the Hindu god of success. That's where my knowledge runs out, I'm afraid.'

'You know the animal ones because you're a vet,' observed Joe.

'I like the female one,' said Aesha. 'She's beautiful.' She was standing in front of a smiling figure holding a flower in two of her four hands and sitting cross-legged in a large lotus flower.

'She is Lakshmi, our goddess of wealth, beauty and prosperity.' A hotel attendant had joined them. He led them along the row of statues and named them all in turn. 'And this is Shiva,' he said when they reached the final statue.

Joe stared at the blue face, the third eye in the middle of its forehead and the cobra round its neck.

'His role is to destroy the universe in order to recreate it,' the attendant explained. Then he added, 'Welcome to our country. I hope you will have an enjoyable stay.'

Chapter 5

Joe was relieved to find cereal and toast on offer for breakfast the next morning. He had enjoyed the meal the previous evening – a selection of different curries that allowed him to pick and choose – but he was ready for something sweeter and more familiar. A local coordinator from the Animal Aid Service, which was closely involved in vulture conservation, had arrived at the hotel in time to join them for breakfast, and Joe watched him tuck into a plate of rice and spicy vegetables with obvious enjoyment. His name was Sachin. He was young and good-looking, sported sunglasses perched on his head, wore jeans and a lumberjack shirt and spoke enthusiastically in impeccable English. Joe immediately decided he was the coolest person he had ever met, especially when Sachin wanted to know all about him.

'How old are you, Joe, and what do you want to be when you grow up?' Sachin asked.

Joe told him he was nine and wanted to be a photographer.

'Nine's a good age,' Sachin responded. 'At nine you can do most things and you can have big dreams.'

Aesha pulled a face. Joe thought she was going to say something derogatory, but she lost the opportunity when Sachin continued, 'When I was nine I wanted to be a pilot or a doctor, but I fell in love with animals and now I'm training to be a vet like your mother.'

'I might be a vet too,' Joe added hastily.

'Then perhaps one day we will be working side by side.'

Sachin grinned encouragingly at him, before

turning his attention to Aesha. Joe was amused to see his sister blush and for once she seemed unsure of herself, though it didn't stop her mentioning that she wanted to swim for her country, an ambition which clearly impressed the young Indian. Joe was keen to regain the spotlight and asked if he planned to fly a kite during the festival.

Sachin shook his head. 'I'll be too busy helping your mother and the other vets and volunteers with the injured vultures. It'll be a very long eighteen hours or more for all of us.'

'No sleep for the virtuous, eh?' said Peter. 'Or do I mean vulturous?'

Aesha groaned loudly. 'You'll have to excuse our father,' she said to Sachin. 'He cracks the worst jokes.'

'Will I be able to help?' Joe aimed the question at his mother, even though he knew what her answer would be.

'No, Joe,' Binti replied. 'From what I

understand, this is a frantically busy time for everyone. There won't be any opportunity for you and Aesha to be involved. Besides, you'll want to be watching the kites.'

'And taking photos,' Peter reminded him.

'Have you ever flown a kite?' Sachin looked questioningly from Joe to Aesha.

Joe shook his head immediately, while Aesha muttered something about having tried to fly one at a friend's house and failing miserably.

'Then you must learn,' said Sachin. 'Tomorrow, if you like, I will show you how.' He sought approval from Peter and Binti.

'That's very kind of you,' said Binti. 'I'm sure they'd love to.'

Joe nodded eagerly. He was excited at the thought of learning to fly a kite in a strange city hundreds of miles from home. This would surely be the start of a big adventure. He secretly hoped Aesha would turn her nose up at Sachin's offer, but she too appeared enthusiastic.

'We'll go tomorrow after breakfast, before

I'm swept away in a flurry of broken wings.' Sachin spoke lightly but frowned at the same time. 'And now I must sweep your mother away to show her where she'll be based during the festival.'

It was then that Joe understood just how much work there was to be done in saving the injured vultures. Binti and the other vets and volunteers would be up all day and all night during the festival and only able to snatch the odd half an hour of sleep in a guest house close to the rescue centre. While he and his father and sister slept in their plush hotel, his mother would be saving birds' lives in what he imagined would be a hot, smelly, crowded room. He wished again that he could be there doing whatever he could to help. *It must be so rewarding being a vet*, he thought. *It must be such a good feeling to save an animal's life.*

'And I'm going to sweep you two away to see the sights of Ahmedabad on a normal day before kite fever takes over,' Peter informed

Joe and Aesha. 'First stop Gandhi's headquarters, second stop a textile museum, third
stop a temple, fourth stop Science City. How
does that sound?'

Joe looked at his sister and could see that she
was as dismayed as he was. It sounded so boring!

All Joe wanted to do was fly kites and help
his mother with the vultures. He had never
heard of Gandhi, and he really wasn't interested in a textile museum. Joe was relieved
when his father said that perhaps they should
save that bit for when Binti could be with them.
He perked up even more when Sachin told
him Science City was structured like a theme
park. He could cope with a temple if it was followed by a thrill ride.

Chapter 6

Ravi was outside the hotel waiting for them bright and early the following morning. 'I will be your driver and guide for the day,' he said.

He obviously relished his role. He took them off the beaten track on the way to the popular sights, so they were able to see people going about their daily lives – hanging out washing, feeding children, scrubbing doorsteps, grinding spices, or simply sitting and watching the world go by. Joe was struck by how poor some of them seemed to be, and felt a bit uncomfortable peering out at them from the plush velour seats of the car. But passers-by waved at them and Ravi wound down his window to chat animatedly with anyone who flagged him down.

'Everyone wants to talk about the kite festival,' he explained to Peter. 'I am telling them to watch out for the vultures and to keep their kites away from them.'

Peter nodded his approval. 'The more people are aware, the greater chance the vultures have of surviving,' he said.

As they drove to Gandhi's headquarters Peter explained that Gandhi was a great Indian leader who had led the struggle for Independence. Joe was shocked by the spartan conditions in which the great leader had lived. He and Aesha were amazed to learn that Gandhi had even refused to eat in protest at the way in which his people were treated. The pictures and photographs that formed a record of his life made them wish the world were a better place. There was even a letter Gandhi had written to Hitler, asking him not to go to war.

'It's a pity there aren't more leaders like Gandhi,' said Aesha, and Joe found himself agreeing.

They continued on, visiting a temple and a mosque, which were completely different both from each other and from any sort of building Joe had ever seen before. The temple was made out of white marble which was so ornately carved that Joe thought parts of it looked like a wedding cake. The mosque had two minarets, which, Ravi told them, would shake if a small amount of pressure were applied to the top of one of them.

'Nobody knows how this happens, but if you shake one minaret, the other one starts to shake as well, even though the passage connecting the two of them remains firm. It's a complete mystery, but it helped them survive a serious earthquake in 2001.'

Joe took one photograph after another, following in his father's footsteps and trying to be creative with angles and shapes as he snapped away at cows sitting in the middle of the road, women carrying baskets on their heads, vegetable vendors with bullock carts and people sitting under canopies weaving garlands of flowers.

'At this rate, I'll have to buy you a new memory stick.' Peter grinned at him. 'When I mentioned there was an amazing photo to be taken every few seconds, I didn't mean you to take every single one.'

When Science City finally opened out ahead of them, it looked like another world.

'It's vast!' Peter exclaimed. 'I didn't expect that.'

Ravi beamed across at him. 'It is a modern jewel in India's crown,' he said proudly. 'Please enjoy.'

Joe couldn't wait to go inside. *This is the coolest-looking place I've ever been to!* Everything was so awe-inspiring. He was more excited than ever when Peter picked up a programme and read out what there was to do. When he listed the thrill rides, Joe was adamant they should start with one of those, but Aesha argued that they should see the musical dancing fountain first.

'What's so great about a musical dancing fountain?' he demanded.

'I think you might be surprised,' their father intervened. 'But just to make things fair, I'm going to choose. Besides, we won't get round everything today, so we'll come back with your mother.'

He strode off in the direction of the Hall of Space, which Joe decided would be all right as a starting point, but which left Aesha dragging her feet in protest.

'Who cares about space?' she grumbled. 'Nobody goes there any more, anyway.'

Even she began to enthuse, though, as they played with robots, entered a lunar capsule, found out what it was like to work in a TV studio and saw how a satellite operated. At every new interactive station, Joe found himself revising what he wanted to be when he grew up. When they went upstairs to the Hall of Science, with its multitude of handles to turn, buttons to press, peepholes to look through and experiments to perform, he was determined that they would come back and spend a whole day in this amazing place.

Once outside again, at Aesha's insistence they made their way to the musical dancing fountain. Joe's jaw dropped when he saw it. This was nothing like he had imagined. Reading from the programme, Peter informed them that it was composed of 113 water jets with 2,073 nozzles. The pond area was massive and the water, which was lit by 935 coloured lights, spurted up as high as a ten-storey building. The water was choreographed to 'dance' to music and light and the whole thing was run by a computer.

'Now do you see what's so great about a musical dancing fountain?' Peter asked Joe.

Joe nodded. He was completely dumbfounded. He took as many photographs as he could, but he knew that none of them could possibly do justice to what he was seeing in front of his eyes.

'Mum would love this!' Aesha cried. 'It's a–ma–zing! I wish I could swim in it.'

'If you do, I won't be the one to fish you out,' chuckled Peter. 'And don't worry, we'll most definitely come back. And now, to finish off a brilliant day for all of us, I think it's time for one of those death–defying simulator rides, don't you, Joe?'

Joe didn't need to be asked twice. He raced ahead in the direction of a large bright-red metal capsule. A short wait later and they were seated inside it, listening to the noise of engines revving loudly. Joe found himself gripping the arms of the seat as they plunged into a volcano at break-neck speed through plumes of smoke and fire. He heard Aesha scream and the squeals of several younger children. It was all so realistic, it was difficult to believe they weren't really surrounded by red-hot lava. Joe turned to his father for reassurance and saw that his father's

36

face was tense as well, which made him want to laugh.

When, after what seemed like hours, the trip was over, they staggered out of the capsule and made their way to where Ravi was waiting for them.

'Have you had a good day?' he asked.

'Exhausting,' Peter replied.

'Brilliant!' Joe and Aesha said.

'I have one more thing to show you,' their guide told them. 'It's on the way home.'

They settled back into the comfort of the Wolseley. Joe struggled to keep his eyes open, even though he was desperate not to miss any of the sights they were passing. He was drifting off to sleep when he felt someone tugging at his sleeve and realised that the car had stopped.

'Look up in the tree,' his father said.

Ravi had got out of the car and was pointing upward. 'Vulture,' he said proudly. 'Always there.'

Joe leapt out of the car, clutching his camera, and stared up through the leaves. There was a large nest of sticks embedded in the fork between two branches and on it sat a vulture.

'Wow!' he exclaimed. 'It's so big!'

He aimed his camera and fired off several shots, just as a blast of warm air peppered him with dust.

'That's an occupational hazard,' observed his father, who was taking his own photographs from the other side of the tree. 'Rain, sun and wind can all wreak havoc in a photographer's life.'

Joe pulled a face and played back the shots he had taken. In one of them, the vulture's wing feathers were displaced by the breeze, making it look curiously misshapen.

'*Feathers in the Wind*', Joe thought to himself. *That's what I'll call that photo.*

'I still think they're ugly,' Aesha muttered, as they returned to the car.

'I hope it'll still be there after the kite festival,' Joe said.

Chapter 7

Binti was already back at the hotel when they returned. Joe couldn't wait to tell her everything they had seen and done.

'The robots and the thrill ride and the musical dancing fountain were so cool,' he said, describing them in detail over dinner. 'And we're going there again with you and – guess what, Mum – we saw a vulture!'

'You did?' Binti asked. 'Do you know where it was?' She aimed the question at Peter rather than Joe, but it was Joe who answered.

'Up a tree,' he replied.

'Helpful,' Aesha groaned.

'Ravi would be able to tell you,' Peter said. 'Is it important?'

'It would be good to know whether or not it's been tagged,' said Binti, 'and what sort it is.'

'How was your day, Mum?' Aesha asked. 'I felt sorry for you having to work while we were having fun.'

'I enjoy my work, so it's not a problem, though I definitely can't go home without seeing Science City after what you've told me.'

'And Lake Kankaria,' Joe added. 'Sachin told me about it and said we should go there for a picnic.'

'And you won't want to miss out on the textile museum,' said Peter.

'It looks like you've got it all mapped out for me.' Binti laughed. 'I'll have to make sure I finish my work in good time. I've been showing the local vets how to deal with the sorts of wounds vultures are likely to receive from the kites and how we can make sure they survive. It's my aim to save every single injured bird.'

'You can do it, Mum,' Joe said confidently, and that night he dreamt of rows of vultures, all of them sporting bandages, including one with an elaborate head bandage that looked like a turban, and all of them nodding their thanks to Binti and her team.

The following morning, Joe woke with a knot of excitement in his stomach. Another day of adventure was opening up before him! Sachin was going to show him how to fly a kite and Sachin was the coolest man on earth. Joe dived out of bed, just as his father appeared through the door from the adjoining bedroom.

'You'd better hurry down to breakfast,' said Peter. 'Sachin's waiting outside for you with a bit of a surprise.'

What sort of surprise? Joe wondered as he scrambled into his clothes.

He arrived in the dining hall to find that his parents had already eaten, but there was no sign of his sister.

'Where's Aesha?' he asked.

'She's tired and has decided to have a lie-in,' said Binti.

'She'll miss out on learning how to fly a kite!' Joe was incredulous. He couldn't believe his sister would prefer to stay in bed than to go out with Sachin.

'Our princess needs her beauty sleep,' said Peter. 'So I shall wait for her to arise while your mother goes off to work and you go off to play.'

Joe was secretly pleased at having a solo kite lesson. He bolted down his scrambled egg on toast.

The surprise revealed itself the moment Joe stepped through the hotel's front entrance. A green and yellow autorickshaw was parked outside. In the driver's seat was Sachin, who jumped up as soon as he saw Joe.

'Are you ready for some fun?' he asked, beaming.

Joe nodded, turning to his father for confirmation that this was all right. Peter had his camera out and snapped him before he knew what was happening.

'Take good care of my son,' he said to Sachin. 'He's the only one I've got.'

'I will take very good care,' Sachin replied.

Joe climbed into the back of the rickshaw and they were off.

The ride was scary and exhilarating at the same time, like being in a bumper car, Joe thought, but – touch wood – without the bumps. Sachin wove his way expertly in and out of the traffic, the rickshaw bouncing and heaving on the uneven road surface. Joe hardly dared look to either side. They passed so close to other vehicles, at times he felt he could stretch out a hand and touch their occupants, especially when they were driving along neck and neck with another rickshaw. Sachin loved using the horn, which was so high-pitched and squeaky Joe doubted anybody could hear it above the cacophony of other noises. He turned occasionally to grin at Joe and shout something about places and people they were passing. Joe struggled to make out what he was saying, but he was thrilled at the magical mystery tour he was being treated to.

Poor Aesha, fancy staying in bed and missing this, he thought as they chugged along a narrow backstreet where chickens skedaddled and children waved excitedly as they passed.

Eventually, they left the city centre behind and came to a vast open area of scrubby grassland. Sachin stopped the rickshaw.

'Here we are,' he said. 'There's plenty of space here for us to practise, though when you're an expert you'll be able to fly a kite from the smallest rooftop.'

He helped Joe from the rickshaw, grabbed a holdall from the front and brought out a red and blue kite that opened into the shape of a diamond. Joe had been hoping for something more elaborate and his disappointment must have been obvious, because Sachin explained that it was best to start with something simple.

'We need to attach the line and then we're ready.'

He showed Joe how and where to tie the string and, once it was secure, handed him the spool.

'This string hasn't got glass on it, has it?' Joe was anxious to know.

Sachin shook his head. 'Don't worry,' he said. 'The vultures are safe with us. Now, hold on tightly to the handles of the spool while I walk away from you with the kite.'

Joe did as he was told, watching the line unravel as Sachin moved away in a direction he had chosen by wetting a finger and holding it up in the air.

'Can you feel the wind blowing from you to me?' Sachin asked him.

Joe wasn't sure he could feel any wind at

all, until a gentle breeze tickled the back of his hair.

'There's not much wind,' he called.

'It's enough,' Sachin called back. 'Now, I'm going to let go of the kite and I want you to pull on the line, not too hard and not too soft. Try to pick up the wind.'

Sachin lifted the kite up as far as he could reach and let go. Joe pulled on the line, willing the kite to fly. It tilted and swayed and plunged to the ground.

'Try again, Joe,' Sachin encouraged him. 'If you feel the kite start to tug, let out some more line.'

Joe tried again and again. The kite resisted his every attempt to get it airborne, until he was left biting his lip with frustration, especially when a group of local children arrived and started telling him where he was going wrong.

'I'm useless,' he cried out. 'I'll never do it.'

He felt like throwing the spool away and demanding to be taken home, but suddenly he felt the kite tugging hard at the line, straining to free itself. This time it was rising upward.

'Let out the line, Joe, let out the line,' Sachin urged him.

Joe allowed the string to roll off the spool and watched the kite streaming up, up into the sky.

'Cool!' he cried. 'Look at it go!'

'Now you can control it by feeding the line in and out,' said Sachin, coming to stand with him. 'Learn to understand how the currents of air move it about.'

For the second time that day, Joe was exhilarated. *I wish Mum and Dad could see me*, he thought, as he manoeuvred the kite so that it dipped and dived and swerved and soared. *I hope they'll buy me my own kite so that I can join in with the festival.*

Chapter 8

They met up with Binti, Peter and Aesha for lunch in a restaurant close to the rescue centre. Joe couldn't help going on about how brilliant the rickshaw ride had been and how he had mastered the art of flying a kite.

'It's not easy,' he assured them. 'It takes a lot of practice.'

'You can show us how,' Binti suggested.

'I would if I had a kite,' Joe immediately responded.

He tucked hungrily into a bowl of chicken biriani and decided he much preferred it to the sandwiches and apple he would probably have had at home. It certainly beat school dinners.

'I thought you might like to visit the rescue centre after lunch,' Binti suggested. 'It's housing a few interesting patients at the moment.'

'Are they all vultures?' Aesha asked.

'Wait and see,' said Binti. 'The vets and volunteers are looking forward to meeting you and showing you their work.'

'I'll be able to take photos, won't I?' Joe said. He was excited at the prospect of photographing wild birds close up.

'I'll pose nicely for you,' Sachin said, pulling a ridiculous face, which made Aesha laugh, despite her attempts to appear aloof and uninterested.

'Let's go then,' said Peter. 'I, for one, am fascinated to see your work.'

They walked the short distance to the rescue centre. The sun was shining brightly and wherever they looked people were chatting animatedly. Even though they had just eaten, Joe was tempted by the delicious smells coming from the street vendors' stalls – a mixture of spicy and sweet and scented. Sitting cross-legged on the pavement, a shoemaker was hammering leather into shape while he sang along to rock music on a radio. Peter asked if he minded having his photograph taken. The shoemaker was delighted and grinned up at him toothlessly.

'I didn't realise he didn't have any teeth,' Peter whispered, chuckling as they walked away.

They reached the rescue centre and Sachin showed them in. It was very clean and modern, not at all how Joe had pictured it. Sachin introduced them to two of the volunteers who were on duty and a young vet called Dipak, who had been working with Binti.

'How's that little monkey of ours?' Binti asked her. 'Still causing havoc?'

'She likes to pull the kittens' tails,' Dipak replied. 'She's very mischievous.'

'Is there really a monkey here?' Joe was thrilled. 'Can we see it?'

'She's called Nanu and she's an orphan,' Binti told him. 'Her mother tried jumping from one tree to another and misjudged the distance. Sadly, she died, but her baby survived. Nanu was only about three days old when she was brought in, but now she's three months and doing very well.'

She led them through a door into a long corridor-like room lined with cages of all sizes. They stopped at each one in turn. Several contained owls, some asleep, some staring out with big watchful eyes.

'They're victims of road accidents,' Binti explained. 'They fly down to catch prey on the verges and aren't quick enough to get out of the way. There will be more here after the festival.'

'They're so beautiful,' said Aesha. 'It's sad they get injured.

'No more sad than the vultures,' Joe protested.

Aesha pulled a face but didn't comment.

51

The next cage contained a fruit bat, which Binti said had got caught up on barbed wire. It had injured not only its wing but its mouth as well, in trying to bite itself free.

'Yuck!' said Aesha when she saw it. 'Bats are the worst.'

'You certainly won't be following in your mother's footsteps,' Peter observed drily. 'It's just as well she doesn't discriminate between different species depending upon how they measure up in the beauty stakes.'

Joe peered into the cage, wanting to like the bat, but he couldn't help agreeing with his sister that there was something disturbingly menacing about its face. And all the stories he'd read recently about vampires didn't help its cause.

'They're fascinating creatures,' Binti said. 'Apart from anything else, they're the only mammal capable of true flight and, despite what you might have heard, they can see almost as well as humans.'

'I thought they used echolocation,' said Joe, pleased with himself at knowing the word.

'Not fruit bats. Some species do, though,' replied Binti. 'Another interesting fact is that a single bat can eat up to six hundred mosquitoes in an hour, so as someone who seems to be a target for the infernal mozzie, I say it's a pity there aren't more of them!'

The following cage contained a cobra. Aesha was about to express her views on it, when Peter jumped in.

'I suppose this makes it on to your list of nasty horrible ugly creatures as well, does it?'

'Yep,' Aesha agreed. 'Snakes are revolting and I don't know why anyone would want to go near one. Can't we go and see the monkey now?'

'What happened to the snake?' Joe asked.

'It had its tail run over,' Binti told him.

They moved quickly past the next few cages, most of which contained cats and dogs, though Aesha stopped to coo at a litter of five kittens.

Another door opened up to an extensive outdoor area where numerous other animals were housed. Binti headed straight for a cage in the centre.

'Here she is,' she said. 'Little Nanu.'

Joe was instantly enchanted. The monkey leapt over to the fence right by them and peered at him curiously, her head cocked to one side. She bounced up and down excitedly and put her hand through the netting as though asking for food.

'Mind your hair,' Binti warned. 'She'll either pull it or check it for anything edible.'

'She's so cute!' Aesha cried. 'Can I hold her?'

Binti shook her head. 'We're trying to limit her contact with humans because when she's ready she'll be reintroduced into the wild.'

Aesha pouted. 'One quick hug wouldn't do any harm.'

Nanu weed just at that moment, causing Aesha to shriek and Joe to fall about laughing.

'It's just as well you weren't hugging her then,' Peter said.

The monkey set off across the cage, squealing loudly as though thoroughly pleased with herself, before returning to hang upside down from her tail in front of her observers.

'She's excited by the attention,' said Binti. 'She won't be so happy when our time is taken up with the vultures and other injured birds. One more day of relative peace, then all hell will break loose.'

Chapter 9

The next day Peter finally let on to Joe that, yes, he would have his own kite to fly.

'What about me?' Aesha had demanded instantly. 'I want my own kite too.'

'You won't know how to fly it,' stated Joe. 'It's not easy. You should have come out with me and Sachin instead of staying in bed.'

'Blah, blah, blah,' growled Aesha. 'I bet it's not that difficult, anyway. You're not just going to buy one for Joe, are you, Dad?'

'Pull a face like that and it won't be the kites causing vultures to drop from the sky,' he remarked.

'Not funny, Dad,' she said. 'And not fair if you buy a kite for Joe and not me.'

They had spent the morning at the hotel. Aesha had gone for a swim, while Joe wandered through the hotel taking photographs and Peter caught up with emails and the newspapers. Binti had left early to visit another rescue centre and work with the vets there.

The hotel was buzzing. Every room was booked and there were guests from all over the world. Joe caught snatches of conversations in languages he could only begin to guess at. The hotel owners had gone to town in decorating the public areas with kites and festoons of ribbons. Even the table decorations were fashioned to represent spools of string.

The mounting excitement was infectious and Joe couldn't wait to set off for the Patang Bazaar, which Sachin had told him was the name for the kite market.

'You must go at night-time to buy,' Sachin had insisted. 'It's the best time. Everybody is there. Everybody is happy. It's an adventure at night-time, especially for young people.'

'We will go at night-time, won't we, Dad?' Joe asked anxiously. 'Sachin says it's an adventure then.'

'We'll go this evening,' Peter promised.

Joe was delighted because it meant his mother could go with them, and he knew he would see precious little of her for the next day or so.

When the evening finally came and his father ordered two autorickshaws to take them to the market, Joe could hardly contain himself while they waited for them to arrive.

'It's fun in a rickshaw,' he said to his parents and Aesha. 'It's a bit scary and noisy because you're so close to the other traffic, but you get used to it.'

'Hark at our seasoned international traveller,' Peter teased him gently.

'For a nine-year-old he *is* a very seasoned international traveller,' Binti said, squeezing Joe's shoulder. 'Not many children his age, or

Aesha's for that matter, will have had so many opportunities to visit other countries.'

'Nor to help save endangered species like we have,' added Joe.

'We haven't exactly done much to help,' Aesha countered.

'You're learning, that's the main thing,' said Binti.

Joe secretly thought that he'd done more to help than his sister. After all, he was the one who'd found an injured tiger in Russia and even now, as he was setting out to buy a kite, he wondered if he might in some way help with the injured vultures.

'Can I have a big kite?' he asked Binti after they had settled into the first of the two rickshaws. 'And can I have one that's not a diamond shape but something a bit different?'

'We'll see what choice there is,' said Binti. 'But you don't want something too big or you'll take off with it!'

Joe imagined himself flying over the city,

weaving in and out of the clouds. *That would be so cool!*

The roads and pavements were heaving as the rickshaws trundled towards the city centre. It was true what Sachin had said, that everybody would be there and everybody would be happy. Men, women and children swarmed in all directions, some already clutching precious purchases, others eagerly spilling in and out of stores in search of their own treasures. Street vendors mopped their brows as they served up one plate of food after another, while queues filled the doorways of restaurants where waiters were run off their feet trying to keep up.

'I don't think I've ever seen so much excitement,' said Binti, and Joe caught the ring of excitement in her own voice.

The rickshaws came to a halt and they clambered out.

'I think everyone in the entire city must be here,' said Peter. 'There's hardly room to move.'

'Stay close to us,' Binti told Joe and Aesha.

'We don't want to lose you.'

'I don't want to get lost!' exclaimed Aesha.

They made their way towards an outdoor stall, its tables covered with an array of spools, ribbons and strings in every size and colour. The stall next to it was the same, the vendors vying with each other to clinch a sale.

'Sachin says homes all over Ahmedabad turn into kite-producing businesses months before the festival, with family members all doing their bit,' Binti informed them. 'The paper and sticks have to be cut, the glue mixed and stirred, and the strings coated with a special glass powder and rice paste.'

'The families must be desperate to see some return for their efforts,' Peter said. 'You can understand why they try so hard to grab your attention.'

'We won't be making our own kites, will we?' Joe was puzzled by the amount of kite-making equipment when the festival was due to start the next morning.

'Not us,' his father assured him. 'But a lot of people obviously will be.'

They came to a central hall, where hundreds of ready-made kites covered the walls, ceilings and countertops. Joe couldn't believe his eyes at how many types there were.

'Wow!' he cried. 'How do we choose?'

There were kites with smiley faces and fierce faces; kites the shape of wind socks, doughnuts, parachutes and sails; kites as small as twenty centimetres, others larger than a metre; kites with one colour, two colours and all the colours of the rainbow. Everywhere they looked, people were asking to take a closer look at one kite, dismissing it and demanding to see another. When they'd made up their mind, they spent the next few minutes haggling over price. The cacophony of voices was so loud Joe could scarcely make himself heard. He wondered how the vendors managed to negotiate with so much din going on, yet they dealt with several people at the same time.

'What do you think, Joe?' Binti had to put her mouth right up to his ear.

Joe felt so overwhelmed he was on the point of

asking his mother to choose for him, when he spotted a blue kite in the shape of a giant squid hanging from a railing by a stall in the corner.

'That one!' he shouted. 'Over there.'

He headed towards it, pushing through the crowds and turning to check that his family was following. As soon as Peter had caught up with him, he pointed again.

'The blue squid,' he said. 'That's the one I'd like.'

'Good choice.' Peter laughed. 'You can't beat a cross-eyed squid.'

He began to haggle with the stallholder and then went through the whole process again when Aesha decided she wanted a multi-coloured arrow-shaped kite from the same place. By the time he had finished he was sweating profusely and desperate to get out.

'In terms of effort expended,' he said as they emerged on to the street, 'these are the most valuable purchases I've ever made. I hope you're happy with them.'

Joe and Aesha nodded. 'Thanks, Dad.'

Chapter 10

Joe and his family ate at a restaurant that evening. The atmosphere was electric with anticipation, everyone talking loudly, some of the diners demonstrating their prowess with a kite through elaborate arm waving and hand gestures.

'If only there wasn't such a big negative side to it all,' Binti sighed. 'I can't quite bring myself to rejoice in their excitement because of that.'

Joe felt a bit guilty that he and Aesha were going to be joining in the celebrations, even though they had bought normal string for their kites. *We won't be doing any harm*, he kept trying to convince himself.

'I only hope the publicity campaign the vets and volunteers have been running will lead to fewer kites flying in the early morning and evening when greater numbers of birds are around,' his mother continued.

'You can't do more than you're doing,' Peter reassured her, 'and for some of these people tomorrow is the highlight of their year. You can't take that away from them.'

'If only vultures weren't quite so endangered.' Binti sighed again.

'I bet you'll save loads of them,' said Joe, trying to cheer her up.

They finished dinner and called for Ravi to take Binti to the rescue centre before returning to the hotel. Joe gave her a big hug.

'We'll miss you,' he said.

Alone in his hotel room, he placed the package containing his kite on a chair and prepared for bed. He didn't like his mother not being with them, even though it happened quite often because of her work. *I wish I could go and help her*, he said to himself. *I'm sure there's something I could do.*

Joe must have fallen asleep, because when he next opened his eyes he could see slivers of daylight through the curtains. He rolled over, unwilling to accept that it might be time to get up. He was still tired from the excitement of the night before. He would wait until his mother or father knocked on the door.

And then he remembered. He leapt out of bed, ran to the window and pushed his way between the heavy curtains. Sunshine streamed into the room, blinding him for a moment, and then he saw.

'Wow!' he cried.

There were kites everywhere he looked and people were flying them from the rooftops. From the seventh floor of their hotel, he had the perfect view. He wanted to open the windows so that he could feel part of it, but the room was air-conditioned and the windows firmly sealed.

'Dad, come here, Dad!'

He ran into his father's adjoining room, which was still in darkness. 'Come and see, Dad.' Joe shook him by the shoulder. 'The kites are flying. It's amazing! There's one that looks like a giant caterpillar.'

Peter looked at his watch. 'Giant caterpillar or no giant caterpillar, I'm not getting up at six-thirty in the morning.'

'Aw, come on, Dad,' Joe persisted. 'It's brilliant. I bet Mum's up already.'

'I shall be grumpy all day,' Peter protested, crawling out of bed nevertheless.

Joe drew the curtains. 'See,' he said triumphantly. 'It's a great view from here. People are flying kites from the roofs of their houses! It's clever the way they can lift them into the air from such a small space.'

Peter stood and looked. 'We certainly

couldn't do that back home,' he observed, 'or we would be the endangered species.'

Joe giggled. 'It's cool to be able to climb up on the roof of your house.'

'I haven't found it cool since I've been here,' Peter joked.

Joe groaned. 'You tell such terrible jokes, Dad.'

'What do you expect at six-thirty in the morning?' Peter replied. 'Can I go back to bed now?'

Joe shook his head, laughing, and grabbed one of the pillows. 'No, I won't let you, and if you try I'll jump up and down on you until you give in.'

'Binti, come back and help me!' Peter cried. 'Your son has stolen my sleep and is threatening me with a pillow.'

Joe threw the pillow at him and for a few moments – to Joe's delight – they indulged in a pillow fight, until they both fell back on the bed exhausted.

'Are you ready to give in and get up?' Joe demanded.

'When your sister wakes, which could be hours.' Peter snorted.

'She's awake. It's difficult not to be with the racket you've been making.' Aesha came into the room through an adjoining door on the other side and walked over to the window. 'Have you seen the kites? They're amazing! And people are flying them from their roofs! Can we go out?'

Joe was delighted and more than surprised to have his sister on his side. He went and stood next to her. Peter, complaining that he didn't have a chance pitted against the two of them, joined them.

'There's the giant caterpillar.' Joe pointed.

Just at that moment, another kite crossed strings with it. The kites' owners tried to free themselves, manipulating the lines one way then the other until, all of a sudden, the caterpillar plunged downward. At the same time, the other kite soared upward in a dance of triumph.

Joe felt a pang of sadness as he watched the caterpillar fall. He hoped his own kite would fare better and was determined to keep it away from any fighter kites. *That's what happens to the vultures*, he thought. *One minute they're flying happily, the next minute they're plunging to the ground*. It was only then that he noticed there were birds in the sky over the city.

Chapter 11

They had already decided that the best place to fly their kites would be from the field where Sachin had taken Joe. They travelled there by autorickshaw at Aesha and Joe's request, and because they knew that Ravi would want to spend the day with his son. The scene that met them on arrival was completely different from when Joe had gone there previously. This time there were groups of people dotted all over the place, some of them guiding kites in the sky, some in the process of launching them, some taking photographs, others simply watching and enjoying the incredible aerodynamic skills of the more expert flyers.

Joe, his father and sister stood for a while and watched, before finding themselves a spot where there was enough room for them to launch their own kites. Joe pulled his squid from its bag and opened it out. He was pleased all over again with his choice, especially since nobody else seemed to be flying a squid.

'Hold it up,' Peter said, and quickly took a photograph of him. 'And you, Aesha.'

Aesha did as she was told, then asked for his help.

'Your brother's the expert,' said Peter. 'What do we do to get your sister airborne, Joe?'

Delighted to be asked, Joe attached a spool to his sister's arrowhead kite and showed her how to roll out the line once the kite was sky-bound. He took the kite from her, licked his finger and held it up, and began to walk away.

'As soon as I let go,' he called, 'pull on the

line, not too hard and not too soft, and try to pick up the wind.'

He let go of the kite. Aesha pulled too hard and it skidded on to the grass.

'More gently,' Joe instructed.

They tried several times, but each time the kite failed to take off.

'Are you sure you're doing it right?' Aesha cried.

Joe could hear the frustration and accusation in her voice, while recognising that she might shortly throw her toys out of the pram and it would be all his fault. *Come on, Joe*, he said to himself. *This time*.

'Once more,' he called. 'The minute you feel the kite start to tug, let out more line.'

He launched the kite into the air and willed it upward. Peter stepped in to help Aesha feel the wind and then, with a sharp whip of its tail, the arrow soared.

'Let out the line, keep letting out the line,' Joe said as he moved to his sister's side.

'Look at it go!' she cried.

'Well done, Joe,' said Peter, picking up Joe's kite. 'Your turn now.'

He copied what Joe had done, moving away from him and then launching the kite into the air. Joe caught the direction of the wind and the giant squid was sky-bound instantly.

'Wow! That's the best yet!' Joe couldn't contain his pleasure at succeeding at the first attempt. 'Look at the way the squid's tentacles are waving.'

'Keep them up there while I take some photos,' Peter said, loading more film into his camera.

Joe was feeling full of confidence and bravado now. He manipulated the line of his kite, shortening it and lengthening it again, giving it quick sharp tugs, then swinging it to and fro.

'I can make my squid dance!' he shouted.

'My arrow's piercing the clouds!' Aesha laughed as she let out more and more line.

Peter videoed them both, then turned his

attention to some of the other kites and their owners. He moved around the field, sometimes taking video footage, sometimes taking still photographs, checking back frequently to see where Joe and Aesha were.

Joe spotted danger from a large black and red kite that had already cut down two others. He wound in his line to move out of the way and accidentally lost the current of air he had been riding. He tried hard to keep the squid flying, but little by little it wafted down to the ground.

'I kept mine up longer than you,' Aesha boasted.

Joe growled inwardly. He was about to look for his father to ask for help to relaunch the squid, determined that this time he would not be beaten by his sister, when a loud squeal made him turn to her instead. She was staring at the sky, where her arrow had become entangled with the black and red fighter kite. In an instant, the fighter kite had severed Aesha's line and the arrow was cut free. It began to fall, not straight down but in fits and starts, drifting further and further away from them over the heads of the crowds.

Joe tried to watch where it was going, but it was swallowed up among the other kites and he could no longer see it.

'Come on, Aesha,' he cried. 'Let's go after it before someone else finds it.'

He quickly rolled up the squid and thrust it into his rucksack, then ran in the direction he had last seen his sister's kite. Aesha followed him. He caught sight of it briefly once, then again. It was drifting towards the network of streets that bordered the field.

'We'd better leave it,' Aesha yelled from somewhere behind, but Joe ran on.

'It can't go much further,' he yelled back. 'You'll be upset if we don't find it.'

He glimpsed the kite one last time as it dropped down among the houses. He came to a halt, trying to work out which street would take him to its landing place. Aesha drew up next to him.

'Did you see where it went?' she asked anxiously.

Joe thought he knew and marched forward. 'This way,' he said. 'It won't be far.'

'What about Dad?' Aesha hesitated before going after him.

'We'll be back before he notices we're not there,' Joe reassured her.

Chapter 12

Once they had left the field and were walking along a narrow side street, Joe felt less confident about where the kite might be. This part of the city seemed to be deserted, with rows of shops and businesses closed for the day. There was nobody about who might help, but they could hear shouts and music coming from several of the rooftops and glimpsed the occasional flash of colour.

They reached another street and hurried down it.

'What if it's landed on one of the roofs?' Aesha said. 'We'll never find it then.'

She's right, Joe thought, *but we can't just give up.*

He felt bad for having been so competitive and wanted Aesha to get her kite back.

A young boy appeared on a pathway that crossed in front of them. He stopped to stare at them and seemed as if he was about to say something, but continued on his way.

'He's probably searching for his kite as well,' Joe observed.

'Come on, let's go back.' Aesha was more insistent. 'Dad will be worrying.'

'Why don't we just look down this street and the next one and then give up if we don't find it?' suggested Joe. 'We won't get lost.'

Aesha agreed reluctantly. 'Two more streets and then we're going back, no argument.'

They walked as fast as they could, scanning doorways and side alleys, until Joe realised it was a hopeless task. There were just too many places where the kite might have gone, and he wasn't even convinced they had set off in the right direction originally. He was on the point of saying so, when he spotted what looked like a pile of old rags quivering by a gatepost. At the same time, he heard a dog bark from somewhere close by.

'What's that over there?' he said, pointing to the shape.

'I don't know,' Aesha replied, 'and I don't care. Let's go. I don't like the dogs.'

'But it moved,' Joe insisted.

He crept slowly towards it. The barking grew louder. All of a sudden, a large black dog appeared a few metres from them on the other side of the shape. It growled threateningly when it saw Joe and Aesha.

They stood totally still, hoping it would go away.

'Come on, Joe,' said Aesha. 'Leave it.'

'It's a vulture, I know it is,' Joe hissed. 'We can't leave it. What would Mum think?'

'We've got to leave it, Joe. That dog's dangerous. It might have rabies.'

Aesha grabbed his arm and attempted to pull him back, which made Joe even more determined to check the vulture was all right. He took the last few steps towards it, aware that the dog was standing its ground just beyond.

'Throw a stone or something to distract it, please, Aesha,' Joe pleaded with his sister.

'That'll make it even more angry,' Aesha replied. 'Please, Joe, let's go. We'll get Dad and come back.'

'I'm not leaving the vulture,' Joe said stubbornly. 'It will die if we leave it. Throw something at the dog to give me time to pick it up.'

He glared at Aesha. She glared back, but bent down and grabbed a potato that was lying in the gutter. She hurled it as hard as she could at the dog. It missed, but the dog, mistaking it for something it might want to eat, hared after it.

'Quick!' Joe cried. 'In case it comes back.'

He leant over the vulture. 'One of its wings has been ripped and there's a cut to its neck,' he muttered.

Joe held the vulture's head and carefully locked his arms round it, surprised at how light and soft it was. Aesha, rather gingerly, helped support it so its beak couldn't hurt them. They began to walk as fast as they could back down the street. They hadn't got far before they heard a menacing snarl behind them. Aesha turned to look.

'The dog – it's coming after us!' she said urgently.

Joe had visions of it leaping at his back and accelerated his pace, worried at the same time that he might be harming the vulture. And then he stopped in his tracks. Ahead of them stood another big dog.

'Oh no!' Aesha wailed. 'Two of them, and we're stuck in the middle.'

Joe was scared now as well. These weren't domestic dogs. They were wild and, from the look of them, very hungry. In rescuing the vulture, Joe had probably taken their first chance of a meal in days. *Perhaps we should dump the bird and run*, he thought. *It probably won't survive, anyway*. But he remembered Binti's determination to save every single injured vulture.

We can't just leave it to be torn apart by wild dogs.

'Up there,' Aesha was shrieking at him. 'Come on, Joe.'

Some concrete stairs led up the side of a derelict-looking building. Aesha was pushing him towards them.

'What if they follow us?' Joe demanded anxiously, but doing as he was told.

'There's a door at the top.'

They clambered awkwardly up the stairs, their progress hampered by concern for the vulture. Below them the two dogs were facing off against each other. Joe listened to the terrible baying and snarling, and was hugely relieved when they reached the door, pushed against it and it fell open. In the nick of time, Aesha closed it behind them, just as one of the dogs hurtled up the stairs.

As they stood there in the semi-darkness, Joe and Aesha could hear the dog scratching at the door, whining continuously.

Joe felt the vulture shudder in his arms. 'Now what do we do?' he said.

Chapter 13

The room they were in was bare, apart from a swivel chair with its springs protruding through the seat and an ink-stained wooden table with only three legs. With some relief, Joe had released the vulture on to the floor. It had struggled momentarily to get away, but collapsed again.

'I think it's very weak,' Joe said to Aesha. 'How long do you think we'll have to wait?'

They had already decided that as soon as the dogs had gone they would escape and fetch help, but the occasional bark and scratching at the door left them in no doubt that it was still unsafe to leave.

Aesha shrugged and sighed loudly. 'We could be here all day at this rate. Dad will be worried sick.'

'What do you think he'll do?' Joe asked.

'He's probably searched the entire field and he'll be going round a second time and a third. It'll be like we've disappeared into thin air.'

Aesha stared out of the small window set in one of the walls, which was the only source of light. One of the panes of glass was broken and let in air, but the window couldn't be opened. Outside, below the level of the window, was a flat roof, but there was nothing opposite except a high solid wall.

'We should never have gone after my kite in the first place without telling Dad,' she said.

'We didn't know this was going to happen,' Joe protested, though he knew deep down that his sister was right. 'We might not have found the vulture if we'd done things differently.'

'Who cares about the stupid vulture?' Aesha snapped. 'We wouldn't be in this mess if it weren't for the vulture. I hated vultures before and I hate them even more now!'

Joe knelt down on the floor and gazed at the bird. He studied its feathers, with their delicate patterns of browns and greys. He took in the shape of its beak, which it used to strip the meat from dead animals, and thought what an extraordinary tool it was. He examined its head, knowing that it was bald for the purpose of cleanliness. *You* are *ugly*, he thought, *but you're beautiful as well, and I'm not going to let you die.*

'It's not the vulture's fault,' he muttered. 'And Mum's a vet and I'm going to be a vet and we should do our best to save endangered species.'

'Not if it means putting ourselves in danger,' Aesha retorted.

'We're not in danger, not really,' replied Joe.

'Try telling that to the dog outside,' snorted Aesha. 'And we're lost as well.'

Are we lost? Joe asked himself. They had

certainly wandered quite some distance from the field, but he was sure they'd be able to find their way back.

They fell silent, partly listening out for the dog and partly because neither of them felt able to say anything, until Joe asked Aesha, 'You'd be sad if the vulture died, wouldn't you?'

Aesha knelt down next to him and stared hard at the bird. 'Yes,' she said after a while. 'I would be sad.'

The vulture stirred a little as if in response and then became still again. Joe scrambled to his feet and went to the window. He could hear voices, faint but persistent. He tried to identify which direction they were coming from. *If we can hear them, can we make them hear us?* he wondered.

'What if we stand here and keep yelling "Help!"?' he suggested. 'Someone's bound to hear us eventually.'

Aesha looked doubtful. 'Everyone's focused on the kites,' she replied.

'What if I could get out of the window?' Joe said. 'What if we break the glass and I climb through it?'

'Then what?' Aesha was curious.

'I shout for help – or . . .' Joe was warming to his idea '. . . or I fly the squid in the hope that Dad sees it.'

Aesha looked doubtful now. 'You'll never be able to fly your kite from such a small space,' she said.

'I can give it a go,' he said simply.

Aesha nodded. 'I'll break the window,' she said. 'I'm stronger than you and you might hurt yourself. Stand clear.'

Joe pulled a face, but he was too pleased that his sister had agreed to want to argue with her. He moved out of the way. Without a second's hesitation, and to his utter astonishment, Aesha picked up the swivel chair and crashed its wheels against the glass, shattering it into a thousand pieces.

'Wow!' was all he could find to say. He

would never have told Aesha, but in that moment she grew in his estimation.

'I'm not just a pretty face,' she said loftily.

Taking great care not to cut themselves, they removed the remaining shards of glass from the window frame and placed the table underneath the gaping hole. Joe grabbed his kite from his rucksack and clambered on to the table. *I'm going to be first out!*

'Wait, Joe.' Aesha held him back. 'What if the roof's not safe?'

Joe hadn't thought of that, but he was certain that flying his kite would be the only way to alert his father to their whereabouts.

'I'll spread my weight until I'm sure it's OK,' Joe promised.

He crawled through the window and once he was on the roof he went down on all fours. He was pleased to discover that the roof was larger than he'd first thought. It seemed to be solidly built as well, with a parapet protecting the edge.

'It's fine,' he called back to Aesha. 'It's perfectly safe.'

He stood up and walked to the parapet. The street below was empty. The surrounding buildings were taller than the building they were in, which meant he was unable to see beyond them. But there were kites in the sky not too far away. *That must be the field over there,* he thought. *Please, Dad, look up here!*

Aesha crawled through the window and joined him. 'Let's give it a try then,' she said. 'I'm worried the vulture's getting worse.'

Chapter 14

The roof might have been bigger than he'd expected, but there was very little space compared to the vast expanse of the field, and there was hardly any breeze because of the tall buildings nearby.

'This is hopeless!' Aesha was close to screaming with frustration after many failed attempts at launching the squid. 'I'm going to see if the dogs are still there.'

Joe watched her climb back through the window and waited, the squid's crossed eyes seeming to mock him. 'Why won't you fly?' he muttered. 'It can't be that difficult.'

It was a few minutes before his sister returned,

the sound of a dog's bark telling him what he needed to know, followed by Aesha's furious face.

'I thought they had gone. I got all the way to the bottom of the stairs and the street was empty, then one came bounding back round the corner,' she said, joining him on the roof again.

'Let's try the kite once more,' said Joe.

'You can't fly a kite without any wind,' Aesha hissed.

'There's the odd current of air,' Joe contended. 'We just need to be patient and make sure we catch it. And we don't have a lot of choice, unless you can think of anything better.'

Aesha snatched the squid from his hands and walked away from him as far as she could go. 'This is never going to work, even if we do manage to launch the kite,' she grumbled loudly. 'Nobody's going to see it.'

Joe told her to hush while he focused on the breeze and ignored it when she pulled a face at him. He asked her to move slightly to her left, a bit further, then a bit further still.

'Make up your mind!' she groaned. 'Are you sure you don't want me to stand on the parapet?'

Briefly, Joe thought that wouldn't be a bad idea, but dismissed it with a wry smile.

'Right, stay there,' he said, 'and when I say "now" I want you to hold the kite above your head and let it go.'

A few seconds later, he shouted his instruction, pulled the line tight and the kite, falteringly, took off. Joe let out more line, slowly but surely. The squid somersaulted and threatened to plunge, then it was ambushed by a strong current of air and swept upward. Joe and Aesha watched with their hearts in their mouths, unable to speak until they were sure it was safely sky-bound.

'We did it!' Aesha clapped her hands with excitement. 'We did it, Joe!'

Joe grinned. He kept releasing more line and could feel the squid trying to escape from him. 'Look at it go!' he exclaimed. 'The wind's so much more powerful up there.'

'Don't take off, will you?'

Aesha laughed, but Joe was finding it difficult to control the kite, it was pulling so hard at
his arms.

'We'll have to make sure we don't let it fall,
and we'll have to keep it out of the way of any
fighter kites,' he said, though what few kites he
could see were too distant to cause a problem.

They took it in turns to hold the squid. Joe
had wanted to do it all himself, but his arms
were already aching so much when Aesha
offered that he was glad to let her play her
part. For a while, they enjoyed the thrill and
challenge of keeping the kite airborne, acknow-
ledging to each other that it was quite a feat and
that they were improving their aerodynamic
skills by the minute.

As time went by, though, Joe became more
and more convinced their plan wouldn't work.
Why should Dad look in this direction? he thought
gloomily. *It may not even be obvious that the squid
is a squid from where he is. He may not even be on
the field any more.*

94

'What if Dad's gone back to the hotel?' Aesha said, handing the spool to Joe. 'It's killing, keeping the kite flying.'

'I don't think he'd go away, in case we came back,' Joe said. 'He'll probably have asked for help.'

'From the police?' Aesha grimaced. 'I hope we don't get into trouble.'

'It's not really our fault,' muttered Joe. He was exhausted, but didn't want to let on to Aesha that he was beginning to think they should just sit and wait for the dog to go. He watched the squid dancing above and listened to the voices coming from below.

Voices! Shouting!

'There's somebody there!' he yelled at his sister.

Aesha ran to the parapet and looked down. 'It's Sachin!' she cried. 'Up here, we're up here.'

Joe was so relieved that he let go of the spool. The squid, free at last, took off with the wind.

Chapter 15

In no time, Sachin and the group of men he was with had frightened off the dog and scaled the stairs to the roof. Joe felt like throwing himself at him he was so joyful.

'We saw the kite,' Sachin told them. 'Your father contacted the rescue centre and asked anyone in the area to look out for you and your kites. He's very, very worried about you.'

Aesha explained what had happened.

'We only meant to be gone a few seconds,' Joe confirmed. 'But we couldn't leave the vulture and the dog wouldn't go away.'

Sachin bent down to examine the bird. 'It's very poorly,' he said, shaking his head. 'We need to get it seen to urgently.'

He took a walkie-talkie from his backpack and made a call to the rescue centre, asking them to send a van and to let Peter Brook know that his children had been found and were fine.

'Does Mum know we've been missing?' Aesha asked.

'We've kept it from her,' Sachin replied. 'She's got enough to deal with at the moment, and your father was certain you'd turn up safe and sound.'

'He won't be very happy when he finds out we've both lost our kites,' Joe said quietly.

'I think he'll be happy just knowing you're OK,' Sachin assured him.

A short while later, the van arrived and the vulture was carefully placed inside. Joe gently patted its feathers. 'Please live,' he said under his breath.

Aesha copied him, saying out loud, 'I hope it lives', and he wondered if she had finally decided that vultures were worth saving.

Sachin walked Aesha and Joe back to the edge of the field, where it had been agreed Peter would meet them. As soon as he saw them, he rushed over and hugged them tight.

'Those were the longest few hours of my life,' he said weakly. 'I knew you would be all right, but I just couldn't imagine what had happened to you.'

'Sorry, Dad,' they both whispered.

Sachin left them to it and returned to vulture duty, while they made their way to a restaurant for something to eat and drink. Joe was so thirsty he devoured a glass of lemonade in one go and demanded another. Above the cacophony of music and voices, Aesha began the story of their escapade, embellishing it somewhat, especially the danger from the dogs.

'You should have seen them, Dad,' she recounted. 'They were both huge and they had froth coming from their mouths. I threw a potato at one of them and because I managed to throw it so far we had time to get the vulture away, otherwise they'd have torn it to pieces, and us as well probably.'

'The kite was my idea,' Joe put in. 'We just hoped and hoped you would see it.'

'Thank goodness you chose a cross-eyed squid, that's all I can say.' Peter smiled. 'If you'd chosen a common or garden diamond, we'd never have found you. Where is the blue beast, by the way?'

Joe bit his lip. 'I'm sorry, Dad, but I let go of it when Sachin arrived,' he said guiltily. 'It was pulling my arms off.'

'Thank heavens,' Peter said, wiping his brow dramatically. 'I've had enough of kites for one day.'

'Does that mean we can't see the *tukals* tonight?' Joe wasn't sure what he thought about that. He'd sort of had enough of kites too, but he didn't want to miss out on the illuminated kites Sachin had mentioned to him when they were together.

'We'll see,' Peter said.

They finished eating and arranged for a taxi to take them back to their hotel. Even Joe didn't feel like a ride in an autorickshaw. All he wanted to do was lie down on his bed and close his eyes. It was only six o'clock in the evening, but it seemed as if they had been awake for twenty-four hours. He wondered how his mother would cope with staying awake all night, and what she would think when she heard about his and Aesha's adventure.

'Will we be able to go and see our vulture tomorrow?' he asked his father as they walked into the hotel.

Peter nodded. 'Your mother had agreed that we should see some of the results of her work, and I think there's even more reason now.'

Stretched out on his bed, Joe played back the events of the day. It had been exciting and exhilarating and scary and exhausting. He was glad Aesha had been with him. He wouldn't have wanted to be on his own to deal with an injured vulture and hungry stray dogs. It had been bad enough when he found himself just metres away from an injured tiger in Russia.

The day wasn't over yet, though. *I'll sleep for a short time, then wake up and go and watch the tukals. Dad won't want to miss them, I'm sure he won't, and if Mum can stay awake, then so can we.*

Chapter 16

Joe didn't wake up, though – not until noon the next day. He was cross when his father came into the room and he realised what time it was.

'Why didn't you get me up?' he complained.

'Because you and your sister were like a pair of Rip Van Winkles,' said Peter, 'and nothing would stir you.'

Joe was about to grumble on, but his father told him to hurry up because they were due at the rescue centre. Joe leapt into action, feeling increasingly impatient when Peter insisted they have something to eat first.

'Have you spoken to Mum?' he asked as they lunched in the hotel. 'Do you know if our vulture's all right?'

'I haven't spoken to her since last night,' Peter replied. 'I'm afraid it wasn't looking too good then. I didn't want to disturb her this morning. They're struggling to cope at the centre with the number of injured birds.'

Ravi was outside waiting for them in his Wolseley.

'Did you enjoy the Uttarayan?' he asked once they were driving along.

Joe and Aesha looked at each other. 'Yes,' they said. 'We had an amazing time.'

'Today everybody will be sleepy and not wanting too much noise.' Ravi laughed.

'I bet!' Peter laughed in reply.

'The vulture I showed you, I looked for it this morning and it's still there in the tree,' Ravi told them. 'When I saw it I thought that is a lucky bird.'

'That's good to hear,' said Peter.

'I waited to fly my kite, you know,' Ravi continued. 'I waited until after early morning and before the evening, and I told all my family and friends they must do the same. I think that bird is still in the tree because we waited.'

'I'll tell the people in the rescue centre,' said Peter. 'Every bird that survives gives hope for the future.'

Every bird that survives gives hope for the future, Joe repeated to himself.

They arrived at the doors of the centre. Joe couldn't wait to see his mother, but he was afraid she might have bad news. He could tell Aesha was tense as well. When they entered, it was noticeable how different the atmosphere was from their previous visit. The vets and volunteers were working flat out to save the many different species of birds that had been caught up in kite strings. Binti was in the centre of it all, dealing with a badly injured owl, while issuing instructions to the younger vets who were bandaging, cleaning, anaesthetising or operating on other wounded birds.

Mum's worn out, Joe thought, when she acknowledged them.

'I'll be with you in a minute,' she said. 'I just need to stabilise this poor chap.'

Joe gazed from one cage to another, searching for the vulture they had saved. Aesha pointed at one sorry-looking bird, but there were quite a few that were similar. Peter had pulled his camera out and was photographing the vets at work and taking close-ups of the injuries they were treating. For once, Joe didn't want to copy him, even when his father explained that the photographs could be used in conservation campaigns. It was all too sad.

At last, Binti finished what she was doing and came to talk to them.

'Thank goodness you're safe,' she said, putting her arms round them both. 'I couldn't believe it when they told me what a scrape you'd got into.'

'We were never in any real danger,' said Aesha, 'but it was a bit scary.'

Joe took a deep breath and asked the burning question. 'Is our vulture all right?'

Binti smiled. 'I told you we would save one hundred per cent of the casualties — and we have. Your vulture's the one over there with the bandaged neck and wing. He'll never fly again, but he wouldn't be alive if you hadn't found him when you did.'

Aesha and Joe stared into the vulture's cage. They were surprised to see that it was on its feet and eating. It stared at them; a knowing stare, Joe thought.

'He's actually quite handsome — in an ugly sort of way,' said Aesha. 'I'm glad we saved his life.'

Binti had to continue with her work, but promised she would be joining them for dinner that evening.

'The worst is over,' she said. 'What I need is food and lots of it, and an early night.'

'And tomorrow is playtime,' Peter reminded her.

'Ah, yes.' Binti nodded her head. 'Science City, a picnic by Lake Kankaria and, best of all, the textile museum, which Dipak assures me is the most fascinating place in Ahmedabad and not to be missed on any account.'

'It's Joe's worst nightmare, isn't it, Joe?' Peter grinned at him.

Joe was still so thrilled that their vulture had been so lucky that he didn't protest. 'I'll survive,' he said.

Zoological Society of London

ZSL London Zoo is a very famous part of the
Zoological Society of London (ZSL).

For almost two hundred years, we have been
working tirelessly to provide hope and a
home to thousands of animals.

And it's not just the animals at ZSL's Zoos in
London and Whipsnade that we are caring for.
Our conservationists are working in more than
50 countries to help protect animals in the wild.

In Nepal and India we are fighting to save endangered
vultures through field conservation projects and providing
veterinary expertise to help care for birds injured during
the kite festival.

But all of this wouldn't be possible without your help.
As a charity we rely entirely on the generosity of our
supporters to continue this vital work.

By buying this book, you have made an essential
contribution to help protect animals.
Thank you.

Find out more at **zsl.org**

Turn the page for a taster of Joe's exciting
adventures on an exotic island in

Shadows under the Sea

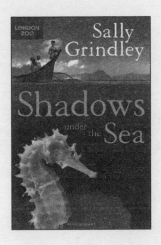

Joe and his family are trying to protect endangered
seahorses in the Philippines – but the fragile
coral reef is threatened by a criminal gang.

Joe has the chance to expose them, but will he
risk his own life to do it?

Chapter 1

'Name the smallest horse in the world,' Peter Brook challenged his two children.

Aesha had just returned from swimming practice. She dumped her bag in the middle of the hall and joined her father in the kitchen. Joe, hearing the sounds of his sister and mother's return, had appeared from upstairs, where he had been doing his homework.

'A pony,' he said.

'Funny, ha, ha!' scoffed Aesha. 'That's not a type of horse – it's just a young horse.'

'No, it's not,' argued Joe. 'A pony is a particular type of horse with a small build. Isn't it, Mum?'

Binti nodded. 'Joe's right, love. You're confusing pony with foal.'

'Shetland, then,' Aesha said sulkily. 'Who cares, anyway?' At thirteen, she was four years older than Joe and didn't like it when he proved her wrong.

'That counts as a pony, and I said pony,' Joe objected.

'You're both wrong.' Their father grinned. 'I'm thinking of something much, much smaller.'

'I know!' cried Joe. 'A seahorse!'

'Correct,' said Peter. 'Go to the top of the class.'

'That's cheating,' Aesha grumbled.

'As my favourite little water baby, I thought you'd be the first to guess.' Peter held a bowl of peanuts out to placate her. 'Now, guess who's been invited to photograph seahorses in the Philippines!'

'And guess who's going with him!' said Binti.

'The Queen,' Aesha suggested.

Her father pretended to cuff her.

'You, Dad? And you, Mum?' Joe questioned.

'Anyone else going?' Aesha asked cautiously.

'Pick your swimming bag up off the floor if you want the answer to be yes,' Binti instructed.

'We're *all* going to the Philippines for four weeks over the summer holidays,' Peter confirmed the minute Aesha had emptied the contents of the swimming bag into the wash and put it away.

'Cool!' said Joe.

'It'll be rather hot, actually!' said his father.

'Even better!' Aesha joined in. She hated the cold, and even though she had enjoyed their recent trip to eastern Russia, where her mother had been invited to work with tiger experts, she much preferred the idea of going somewhere hot.

'What will you do while we're there, Mum?' Joe asked.

'I hope to learn a little more about seahorses,' she replied. 'They're not something I've ever had to deal with. However, since more and more people are keeping them in aquaria —

because they're cute – it might be as well if I were better informed.'

Binti was an international wildlife vet who worked locally with sick animals, and regularly travelled overseas to lend her expertise where it was needed.

'I bet the seahorses don't like being kept in aquaria very much,' said Joe.

'Unless you're a real expert, they're very tricky to look after,' replied Binti. 'Seahorses are fussy eaters and get sick and stressed very easily, especially if they don't have somewhere to hide or are put in with other fish that take their food.'

'People are so dumb,' said Aesha. 'Why do they have to turn every animal into a pet?'

'It's one of the reasons they're becoming endangered,' Binti said.

'What, people?' Peter grinned.

'Bad joke, Dad,' said Aesha. 'Will we be able to go snorkelling?'

He nodded. 'Of course – you'll be like a

couple of beetles scuttling around on top of the water.'

'How long is the flight to the Philippines?' Joe wanted to know.

'It's around twelve hours to Hong Kong, and then another two and a half hours to Cebu,' said Binti.

Joe groaned. 'I hate long flights – they're so boring, and I can never get to sleep.'

'That's because you spend your time imagining that everyone else is up to no good.' Peter laughed.

'That's not true,' Joe protested. 'Just because I thought someone on a plane was a smuggler once . . .'

'When are we going?' Aesha asked.

'Two days after you break up from school. You children just don't know how lucky you are.'

Joe looked at his father. He thought he probably *did* know how lucky they were – his friends told him often enough. It would have been easy to think that everyone travelled to far-flung corners of the world on a regular basis considering his family's lifestyle, but his friends assured him that wasn't the case.

'Poor Foggy will be off to the doggery again, I suppose,' Joe said, pushing his bottom lip out sadly.

'Poor Foggy will be off to Waggy Tails Boarding Kennels, as usual, where he'll be seriously pampered and spoilt, leaving your mother and me teetering on the edge of bankruptcy.'

'As an endangered species, I'm sure the seahorses will be very grateful for any sacrifices Foggy makes on their behalf,' Binti replied, smiling.

Chapter 2

Since his father's announcement, Joe had been counting down the days to their trip and now, the day before they were due to leave, he was amazed to discover that the Philippines were an archipelago of over seven thousand islands in the Pacific Ocean. He hadn't given it much thought until then.

'Only four thousand are lived on,' his father told him. 'The rest are too small or are uninhabitable.'

'Will we stay on just one of them?'

'We'll stay for several days on Jandayan Island, which is where many of the studies on seahorses are being carried out, and then we'll go island-hopping.'

'Cool!' said Joe.

Binti explained that there were at least forty species of seahorse in the world.

'The largest is the big-belly seahorse, which is about the size of a banana, while the smallest is Denise's pygmy, which is about the size of a pine nut.'

'I can tell you something about seahorses too,' said Aesha. 'It's the male that gives birth to the babies and he carries them in his pouch.'

'Quite right,' Binti agreed. 'Depending on the species, he can be pregnant from nine to forty-five days, and may have between five and two thousand babies in his pouch.'

'Two thousand!' Joe exclaimed.

'I know something else,' said Aesha proudly. 'Seahorses mate for life.'

'Ah, isn't that nice,' said Peter. 'Just like your mum and me. Though when she gives me one of her scary looks, I wonder if I haven't made a big mistake.'

Binti gave him a scary look and chased him with a tea towel. Joe joined in, pulling the worst face he could, and Foggy, their schnauzer, woken by the excitement, scurried round Peter's legs, barking loudly.

'I knew it! My son's taking after his mother, and even the dog's against me,' Peter cried dramatically. 'I bet a big-belly seahorse doesn't have to put up with such treatment. I'll have to retire to my shed for a bit of peace and quiet.'

'A seahorse doesn't have a shed to retire to,' Aesha observed.

'More like a stable!' Joe chortled. 'Ha!'

'You're all mad,' said Binti, 'and I'll be hopping mad if you don't hurry up and finish packing.'

'Do you mean island-hopping mad?' Joe said, grinning.

'Ha, funny, ha,' said Aesha. 'You and Dad tell the worst jokes.'

'Nobody would think we were going away for a month tomorrow morning from the state of your rooms,' said Binti in exasperation. 'Now move!'

'It's that scary face again,' Peter said.

Binti picked up a broom and swept them out of the kitchen.

Joe ran to his bedroom, shoved his model-making kit under the bed, grabbed his underpants, T-shirts and shorts from the drawers and dumped them in the case Binti had left out for him. He took his camera from the shelf, wrapped it in a towel and placed it carefully in a corner of the case. Then he picked up his flip-flops and a pair of sandals and threw them in on top. He could hear Aesha complaining that her suitcase was too small to accommodate everything she needed, and his father replying that she wouldn't require her ball gown and tiara where they were going.

Joe was incredibly excited. He had been on plenty of trips with his parents before, but this one promised to be particularly fascinating, and he would have plenty of opportunities to take photographs like his father. He loved travelling on boats and he had never snorkelled before, so that was something else to look forward to. There was also something very appealing about seahorses that made him eager to see them in their natural environment. He laid his brand new flippers and snorkel mask in the suitcase, hoping that this was going to be his best adventure yet.

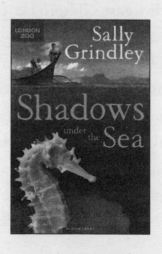

OUT NOW